LEA...

JONA... ...AMES

SAYS

"School's Out!"

by Crystal Bowman
illustrated by Karen Maizel

ZondervanPublishingHouse
Grand Rapids, Michigan

A Division of HarperCollins*Publishers*

Jonathan James Says, "School's Out!"
Text copyright © 1997 by Crystal Bowman
Illustration copyright © 1997 by Karen Maizel

Requests for information should be addressed to:

☵ Zondervan Publishing House
Grand Rapids, Michigan 49530

Library of Congress Cataloging-in-Publication Data

Bowman, Crystal.
 Jonathan James says, "School's out!" / written by Crystal
Bowman; illustrated by Karen Maizel.
   p. cm. — (Jonathan James)
 Summary: Although Jonathan James doesn't want school
to end because he will miss his friends, he finds that going
fishing and attending summer Bible camp are also fun.
 ISBN 0-310-21209-X (softcover)
 [1. Rabbits—Fiction. 2. Summer—Fiction. 3. Christian
life—Fiction.] I. Maizel, Karen, ill. II. Title. III. Series:
Bowman, Crystal. Jonathan James.
PZ7.B6834Jw 1997
[E]—dc21   96-29652
                   CIP

Printed in the United States of America

97 98 99 00 01 02 /❖ DP / 10 9 8 7 6 5 4 3 2 1

To my friend Helen,
who enjoyed summer vacation
as much as I did

—C. B.

For my father, Harold,
who always showed me in which
direction to cast my line

—K. M.

CONTENTS

THE LAST DAY OF SCHOOL

It was the last day of school.
Jonathan James gave Mrs. Morris
a shiny red apple.
"Thank you, J.J.," said Mrs. Morris.
"I will miss you," Jonathan said.
Jonathan liked school,
and he liked Mrs. Morris.
He did not want school to end.

"First we will clean out our desks," said Mrs. Morris.
"Then we will go outside."
Jonathan's classmates cleaned out their desks.
Jonathan didn't.

"What's wrong, J.J.?"
asked Mrs. Morris.
"I will miss coming to school,"
said Jonathan.
"If you take your books
and pencils home,
you can pretend you are at school,"
said Mrs. Morris.
"Good idea!" said Jonathan.

He put his books and pencils
in his tote bag.
Then Jonathan went out to play.

First he played tag with Matt.

"You're it!" said Matt.

"I will miss playing tag with you,"
said Jonathan.

"But if you come home with me,
we can play tag at my house.
We will pretend we are at school."

"Okay!" said Matt.

Next, Jonathan played on the swings with Mandi.

They swung back and forth.

"I will miss swinging with you," Jonathan told Mandi.

"But if you come home with me, we can swing at my house.

We will pretend we are at school."

"Oh, boy!" said Mandi.

"That will be fun."

Then Jonathan played ball
with Jason and Chris.
Jonathan threw the ball to Chris.
Smack! Chris hit the ball.
"I got it!" cried Jason.
"I will miss playing ball with you,"
Jonathan told Jason and Chris.
"But if you come home with me,
we can play ball at my house.
We will pretend we are at school."
"Okay," said Jason and Chris.

Soon it was time to go home.

"Good-bye," said Mrs. Morris.

"Have a nice summer."

"Would you like to come to my
house?" asked Jonathan.

"We can pretend we are at school."

Mrs. Morris smiled.

"Oh, yes!" she said.

"That would be nice."

So everyone walked home
from school with Jonathan.
Jonathan was happy.
He had his books and pencils.
He had his friends.
And he even had his teacher.

"Summer will be fun,"
said Jonathan,
"just like school."

THE FISH SUPPER

Jonathan got up early.

He and Father were going fishing.

They drove to the lake.

"I hope we catch some fish
for supper," said Jonathan.

"A fish supper would be nice,"
said Father.

Father picked up a box.

"Here, J.J.," he said.

"You may carry the worms.

I'll take the poles."

They walked to the boat.

Jonathan tripped and fell.

"Oh, no," cried Jonathan.

The worms went everywhere.

They began to crawl away.

Father got them just in time.

He put the worms back in the box.

"We won't have a fish supper
without worms," said Father.

18

Then Jonathan and Father
got in the boat.
They rowed to the middle
of the lake.

"It's time to fish!"
shouted Jonathan.

"Shhh," whispered Father.

"We won't have a fish supper
if you scare them away."

"Sorry," said Jonathan.

Father put a worm
on Jonathan's hook.
"Put it in the water," he said.
Jonathan tried to put it
in the water.
But the hook caught on his pants.

"Help!" cried Jonathan.

"Oh, dear," said Father.

"We won't have a fish supper
if your hook isn't in the water."

Finally, Jonathan's hook
was in the water.
He sat and waited.
"I got one!" shouted Father.
Father reeled in his fish.
"It's a big one!" shouted Jonathan.

Father put it in the pail.

"That's one for supper," said Father.

Then Jonathan felt a tug.

"I got one, too!" he shouted.

Jonathan reeled it in.

"That's two for supper,"
said Jonathan.

Jonathan and Father fished
all morning.
Soon the pail was full.
It was time to go home.

"We have lots of fish for supper,"
said Father.

But Jonathan started to cry.

"I don't want to eat the fish,"
he said.

"I want to put them back."

"Are you sure?" asked Father.

"We won't have a fish supper
without fish."

"Yes, I'm sure," cried Jonathan.

"All right," said Father.

Father put the fish back in the lake.

"I spoiled everything,"
Jonathan said sadly.

"No, you didn't," said Father.

"We had fun catching fish together.
That's the important thing."

On the way home,

Father stopped at the grocery store.

Jonathan found a box of crackers.

They were shaped like fish.

"Look!" said Jonathan.

"We can have a fish supper after all."

Father smiled.

"Yes," he said.

"A fish supper would be nice."

JONATHAN GOES TO
BIBLE CAMP

Mother was helping Jonathan pack.
He was going to Bible camp
for two whole days.
"I wish my friends were
going with me,"
Jonathan told Mother.

"You will meet new friends,"
Mother told him.
"What if I don't like them?"
asked Jonathan.
"If you try, you can like anyone,"
said Mother.

Mother, Father, and his
little sister, Kelly,
brought Jonathan to camp.
There was a cabin and a pond.
And there were lots of kids.
"Hello, J.J.," said the camp leader.
"My name is Joey, and this is Ricky.
He is your camp buddy.
You will look out for each other."

"Let's go for a canoe ride,"
said Ricky.

"Oh, boy!" said Jonathan.

Jonathan put on a life jacket.

He liked riding in the canoe.

Then Ricky rocked back and forth.

"Stop that!" shouted Jonathan.

Splash! The canoe tipped over.

"Look what you did!"

Jonathan sobbed.

"Now I am cold and wet!"

34

Joey helped Jonathan and Ricky
out of the cold water.

"Put on dry clothes," he said.

"I will make a fire."

Jonathan and Ricky changed
their clothes and sat by the fire.
"Hot dogs for dinner!" Joey shouted.
Jonathan was hungry.
"I will cook our hot dogs,"
said Ricky.

He put the hot dogs on a stick
and cooked them over the fire.
"Oh, no!" cried Jonathan.
"You burned our hot dogs!"
Jonathan ate his burned hot dog
with lots of ketchup,
but it still tasted bad!

Soon it was time for bed.

Jonathan and Ricky went

to the cabin

and put on their pajamas.

"I get the top bed," Ricky shouted.

Jonathan wanted the top,

but he got in the bottom bed.

Ricky wiggled and wiggled.

"Lie still!" Jonathan told him.

Jonathan closed his eyes.

Boom! He heard a loud noise.

"What was that?" asked Jonathan.

"It was me," said Ricky.

"I fell out of bed!"

"Oh, Ricky!" said Jonathan.

"You tipped over the canoe.

You burned the hot dogs.

And now you fell out of bed."

Ricky started to cry.

"I didn't mean to," he cried.

"I'm sorry."

Then Jonathan felt bad for Ricky.

"It's okay," he said.

"Maybe tomorrow will be better."

"Can we switch beds?" asked Ricky.

"Sure," said Jonathan.

Jonathan climbed in the top bed.

Ricky got in the bottom bed.

Jonathan closed his eyes
and said his prayers.
"Dear Jesus," he whispered,
"Please be with Ricky and me.
Help us have a better day tomorrow.
Amen."

The next day, Jonathan and Ricky
went for a canoe ride.
Ricky sat still.

Jonathan cooked the hot dogs
just right,
and Ricky burnt the marshmallows.
"They taste better that way,"
he said.
Jonathan laughed.
"Yes, they do," he agreed.

"You are a good buddy,"
Ricky told Jonathan.
Jonathan put his arm around Ricky.
"So are you," he said.

Make Jonathan James your friend!

Jonathan James Says, "I Can Be Brave!"

Jonathan James is afraid. His new bedroom is too dark. He's going into first grade. And he has to stay at Grandma's overnight for the first time. What should he do? These lively, humorous stories will show new readers that sometimes things that seem scary can actually be fun!

ISBN: 0-310-49591-1

Jonathan James Says, "Let's Be Friends!"

Jonathan James is making new friends. In four easy-to-read stories, Jonathan meets a missionary, a physically challenged boy, and a new neighbor. New readers will learn important lessons about friendship and that friends like us just for who we are.

ISBN: 0-310-49601-2

Jonathan James Says, "I Can Help!"

Jonathan James is growing up, and that means he can help! In four stories written especially for new readers, Jonathan learns to pitch in and help his family—sometimes successfully and sometimes not. Young readers will learn that they can help, too!

ISBN: 0-310-49611-X

Jonathan James Says, "Let's Play Ball!"

Jonathan wants to learn how to play baseball. But who will teach him? Will he ever actually hit the ball? Fun-filled stories will teach young readers that, with practice, they can succeed in whatever they try.

ISBN: 0-310-49621-7

Jonathan James Says, "School's Out!"

Hurrah! Jonathan James makes it through the last day of school and gets to spend the summer fishing with his father. He even goes on a trip to Bible camp! In short stories that new readers will love, Jonathan learns how to be flexible ... and your young reader can too!

ISBN: 0-310-21209-X

Jonathan James Says, "I Can Hardly Wait!"

Waiting is hard, especially for Jonathan James! When Jonathan receives new roller blades from his dad during the winter, can he wait until spring before trying them out? Beginning readers will enjoy three humorous stories—and they'll learn about patience along the way!

ISBN: 0-310-21207-3

ZondervanPublishingHouse
Grand Rapids, Michigan 49530
http://www.zondervan.com

Crystal Bowman was raised in Holland, Michigan, where she enjoyed many summer days on the beaches of Lake Michigan. She also enjoyed spending time at their cottage where she often went fishing. "I caught perch and blue gills and baited my own hook!" she says. Crystal now lives in Grand Rapids, Michigan, with her husband and three children.

Karen Maizel enjoys studying people when they're not looking. She remembers the looks on their faces, or the way their knees bend, and uses what she learns from them in her drawing. "I do this even when I draw bunnies," she says. She lives near Cleveland, Ohio, with her husband and three children.

Crystal and Karen would love to hear from you. You may write them at:

Author Relations
Zondervan Publishing House
5300 Patterson Ave., S.E.
Grand Rapids, MI 49530